T-Rex Seeks

Written by Charlotte Raby

Illustrated by James Cottell

Collins

T-Rex seeks

Yinlong near the rocks

T-Rex seeks

Yinlong near the rocks

Yinlong howls

T-Rex looks down

Yinlong howls

T-Rex looks down

Yinlong in the soil

T-Rex joins him

Yinlong in the soil

T-Rex joins him

 Review: After reading

Use your assessment from hearing the children read to choose any GPCs, words or tricky words that need additional practice.

Read 1: Decoding

- Use grapheme cards to make any words you need to practise. Model reading those words, using teacher-led blending.
- Ask the children to follow as you read the whole book, demonstrating fluency and prosody.

Read 2: Vocabulary

- Look back through the book and discuss the pictures. Encourage the children to talk about details that stand out for them. Use a dialogic talk model to expand on their ideas and recast them in full sentences as naturally as possible.
- Work together to expand vocabulary by naming objects in the pictures that children do not know.
- Read pages 2 and 3. Ask: What similar word or words could we use instead of **seeks**? (e.g. *looks for*) What else is Yinlong **near**? (e.g. *trees, ferns, butterflies, dragonfly*)

Read 3: Comprehension

- Discuss dinosaurs and encourage the children to describe their favourite dinosaurs or to retell any dinosaur stories they are familiar with.
- Reread pages 6 and 7. Ask questions about what has happened: Why do you think Yinlong **howls**? (*Yinlong falls*) Why do you think T-Rex **looks down**? (e.g. *to see if Yinlong is hurt*)
- Turn to pages 14 and 15. Ask: Do you think Yinlong and T-Rex are friends? Why? (e.g. *yes – they played together*) In what ways are they the same? (e.g. *they both live near rocks and ferns; they both fell in the soil*) In what ways are they different? (e.g. *T-Rex is big, Yinlong is small, T-Rex is green, Yinlong is blue*)